KEEP RUNNING, ALLEN!

KEEP RUNNING, ALLEN!

by Clyde Robert Bulla

Pictures by Satomi Ichikawa

Thomas Y. Crowell Company, New York

Copyright © 1978 by Clyde Robert Bulla   Illustrations copyright © 1978 by Satomi Ichikawa

Library of Congress Cataloging in Publication Data

Bulla, Clyde Robert.   Keep running, Allen!

SUMMARY: The youngest in the family, Allen seems to be always running after his ever-active sister
and brothers until he discovers the satisfaction of just being quiet and observing things around him.
[1. Brothers and sisters — Fiction] I. Ichikawa, Satomi. II. Title.
PZ7.B912Ke   [E]   77-23311
ISBN 0-690-01374-4   ISBN 0-690-01375-2 (lib. bdg.)

10 9 8 7 6 5 4 3 2

To Allen

Allen had a sister and two brothers.
Jenny was the oldest. Then came Mike and
Howard. Allen came last.
   He was the youngest and the smallest.
   Every day they played up and down the street.

Mother told Allen, "Stay with your sister and brothers."

But Jenny and Mike and Howard went too fast. They had lots of places to go, and they never stayed anywhere very long.

By the time Allen caught up with them, they were off again.

"Hurry up, Allen!" they would call back to him. "Keep running, Allen!"

One day they heard that the ice-cream man was giving
away free samples. They ran after the ice-cream truck.
"Run, Allen," said Mike. "Hurry up."

But the ice-cream man wasn't giving away free samples.

They saw old Mr. Feather on his way to mail a letter.
"Let's go help him," said Howard.
"Come on, Allen," said Jenny. "Keep running."

She and Mike and Howard helped Mr. Feather mail his letter.

Then Mike said there was a monkey up a tree in the next block. "I think it got out of the zoo," he said.

"Don't stop," Howard called back to Allen. "Hurry up!"

They all ran to the next block. But it wasn't a monkey up the tree. It was only a boy looking for birds' nests.

They chased a big dog.

"Maybe it's lost," said Jenny. "If we catch it, we might get a reward."

They chased it as far as the park, and it got away.

All the time Allen had been running after them. He
didn't catch up till they stopped at the park.
Then they didn't want to stay.

"Let's go home," said Mike. "I want to get my bike."

"I want to get mine, too," said Howard.

"If we'd had our bikes," said Jenny, "that dog wouldn't have got away."

And the three of them were off again.

Allen was hot and out of breath, but he started after them. He stepped on his shoelace and fell down.

He lay there. The grass felt good.

"Allen!" called Jenny.
"Allen!" called Mike and Howard.

He didn't move. There was a fuzzy green worm in the
grass. He wanted to see if it would crawl over his hand.
He lay very still, and it did crawl over his hand.

A bluejay scolded him. He waved at it, and it flew away.

He looked at the sky. There were white clouds, and he could see things in them. He saw a funny face—and a chicken—and a woman in a chair.

He heard Jenny say, *"Allen!"*

He heard Mike say, "Where is he?" and Howard said, "There he is."

They had come back.

Jenny said, "What's the *matter* with you? Get up."
He looked at them. He didn't get up.
"Let's just leave him," said Mike.
"We're going to leave you, Allen," said Howard.
"We *can't* leave him," said Jenny. "Get up, Allen."

But he didn't get up.

"Don't be stubborn," said Jenny.

"You look like a big old slug, Allen," said Mike. "This is how you look."

He went limp and flopped down onto the grass.

He said, "This is soft."
"What is soft?" asked Howard.
"The grass," said Mike. "It's soft as a bed."
Howard tried it. He lay on his back. "It *is* soft. And it smells like — it smells like *grapes*."

"More like watermelons," said Mike.
"It does not!" said Jenny.
"You can't tell from up there," said Howard.

Jenny lay down. She leaned back. "Maybe it is a little like grapes. A little like watermelons, too," she said. "Oh, look up there! Look at that cloud. It's a frog."

"Now it's turning into an old shoe," said Mike. "Look up at the sky and shut your eyes a little. Doesn't it make you feel — dreamy?"

They lay there for quite a while. They stopped talking and just looked at the sky. They all lay in a row, and it was the best time Allen had ever had.